This book is dedicated to my fourth-grade teacher, Kate Millonzi,
the first to love me back. —T.M.

To all of the teachers who remind us that life goes beyond the textbooks
and test grades and who teach us not only how to be great students
but, first and foremost, how to be great humans —E.R.

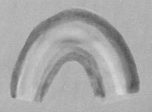

Text copyright © 2023 by Taylor Mali
Jacket art and interior illustrations copyright © 2023 by Erica Root

Visit us on the Web! rhcbooks.com

Educators and librarians, for a variety of teaching tools, visit us at RHTeachersLibrarians.com

Library of Congress Cataloging-in-Publication Data
Names: Mali, Taylor, author. | Root, Erica, illustrator.
Title: The teachers I loved best / written by Taylor Mali ; illustrated by Erica Root.
Description: First edition. | New York : Doubleday Books for Young Readers, [2023] | Audience: Ages 4–8.
Summary: Illustrations and rhyming text celebrate the special teachers who make a difference in our lives.
Identifiers: LCCN 2022005786 (print) | LCCN 2022005787 (ebook)
ISBN 978-0-593-56523-0 (hardcover) | ISBN 978-0-593-56524-7 (library binding) |
ISBN 978-0-593-56525-4 (ebook)
Subjects: CYAC: Stories in rhyme. | Teachers—Fiction. | LCGFT: Picture books. | Stories in rhyme.
Classification: LCC PZ8.3.M3 Te 2023 (print) | LCC PZ8.3.M3 (ebook) | DDC [E]—dc23

MANUFACTURED IN CHINA
10 9 8 7 6 5 4 3 2 1   First Edition

The TEACHERS I LOVED BEST

Written by **TAYLOR MALI**

Illustrated by **ERICA ROOT**

Doubleday Books for Young Readers

Easy teachers who gave easy tests
are not the teachers I loved the best.

No, I loved the teachers who made me work hard
in the classroom, the science lab,
    the theater, and the schoolyard.

Those are the teachers who stand out from all the rest.

Those are the teachers that I loved the best.

And they loved me, too, even at my worst.
In fact, I think they may have loved me first.
And gave me what I needed, and had my back,
and sometimes pushed it gently
        just to keep me on track.

Sure, the best teachers can be demanding,
but always with the goal of commanding understanding.
Are there errors in your work?
See if you can spot them.
'Cause right answers aren't important
if you don't know how you got them.

I had a science teacher once who had us put on a play
about the solar system and the intricate way
that the planets and their moons revolve around the sun.
Did you know that Jupiter has many moons?
You will (because you are one).

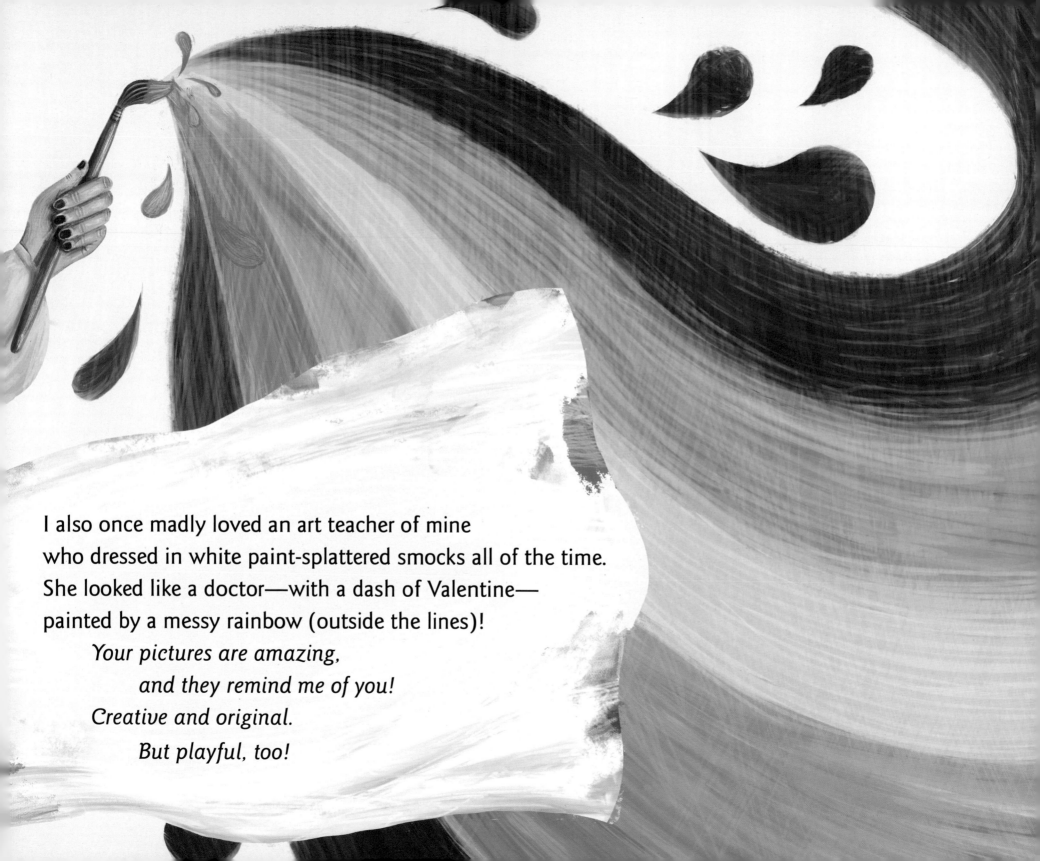

I also once madly loved an art teacher of mine
who dressed in white paint-splattered smocks all of the time.
She looked like a doctor—with a dash of Valentine—
painted by a messy rainbow (outside the lines)!

> Your pictures are amazing,
> and they remind me of you!
> Creative and original.
> But playful, too!

I've been lucky with every music teacher I've had
even though my singing voice
is what you might call . . . *bad!*
    You're off-key again,
        but I couldn't be prouder,
    the way you make up for it
        by singing even louder.

What I've loved about my favorite teachers in the end
is how each one became so much more than a friend.

They requested the best of me on almost every day.
Like a coach before a big game might gather the team and say,
  You won't win every game,
      but neither will you lose today
  if everyone gives everything
      on every single play.

Even now those words still fortify and fire me.
The teachers I loved best knew just how to inspire me.

Let me interrupt myself in case I forget to mention
that not all teachers teach by being the center of attention.

If something gives you trouble, some teachers coach you through it.
Or they build your confidence until you feel there's nothing to it.
Or whisper from the back row,
     I know that you can do it!

Here's one of the most curious features.
Those great educators? They're not always teachers.

They can be principals, librarians, or crossing guards.
A great teacher is anyone who makes you work hard—
harder than you ever thought you could—
who makes you want to be *better* than
      just . . .
           plain . . .
               good.

My favorite teachers always went
    beyond and above for me,
and I thrived in their classes
    'cause I knew that they had love for me.

And love is at the center of every great teacher's lesson.
If you've ever had one, then you know they've been a blessing.

Let me say it simply as a matter of fact:
I loved the teachers I loved best . . .

. . . because they loved me back.